I0764606

THE SOUND OF NAKED SPURS:
A SPAGHETTI WESTERN SCREENPLAY

KARL SMITH

Published by orphic house
* UNITED KINGDOM *

THE SOUND OF NAKED SPURS:
A SPAGHETTI WESTERN SCREENPLAY

Published by 

First published in Great Britain by
Orphic House
95 Longhirst, Middlesbrough TS8 0TD
Creative Director: Karl Peter Smith

First Edition-Hardback with dust Jacket-January 2011

Writers Guild of America, west, Inc.
NAKED SPURS
By KARL PETER SMITH - writer
Registration #: 1236492
Effective Date: 10/29/07

Library of Congress
United States Copyright Office
101 Independence Avenue SE
Washington, DC 20559-6000
Registration Number: PA 1-607-940
Effective date of registration: August 28, 2008
Performing Arts title: Purge the Soul

The British Library
Legal Deposit Office
Boston Spa, Wetherby
West Yorkshire
LS23 7BY
Deposit: January 2011

Orphic House

British Library Cataloguing in Publication Data

Smith, Karl Peter.
The sound of naked spurs : a spaghetti western screenplay.
1. Miwok Indians--California--Drama. 2. California State Prison at San Quentin--Drama.
I. Title
822.9'2-dc22

ISBN-13: 978-0-9566156-8-8

Also available in PAPERBACK - under the original title
ISBN-13: 978-0-9566156-2-6 *Naked Spurs: Screenplay*

DOWNLOAD
www.lulu.com

'Encourage the turning of a page.'
- Orphic House

SPECIAL ACKNOWLEDGEMENTS

Special thanks to

Johanna Davidson
(Johannesburg, Gauteng, South Africa)

And a post'humous CELEBRATION of a life;
the holy man:

Sitting Bull

- Hunkpapa Lakota Sioux

Born: Grand River, South Dakota

NAKED SPURS

"NO ONE GETS THEIR DRAWERS OFF FASTER IN THE WEST"

CALIFORNIA 1876

A COAST MIWOK WARRIOR
AND THE PRISON THAT WAS TO BE NAMED AFTER HIM

Saint ...  *... Quentin*

A YOUNG ARTIST creates a Wild West diorama and tells the seriously tall tale of NAKED SPURS, his great-great grandfather.

NAKED SPURS is the **plausible** tale of the BEAT THE BOUNTY competition a contest attracting the fastest guns in the West to the largest manhunt in history.

As the streaking inmate of San Quentin penitentiary NAKED SPURS must run for life along with other criminals.

This is one story he cannot run away from.

"FROM THE MAN WITH BALLS IS BORN A LEGEND."

Inspiration:

Wyatt Earp told his memoirs to his biographer Stuart Lake.
In one story he was suspected of fixing a prize fight in which he was the judge.
The book was suspected to be entirely fictional.

Concept:

'*The Good, the Bad and the Ugly*' meets '*My name is Earl*' ... well, Earp actually.

(from the rear cover of paperback)

"WYATT EARP"

Part one.

WYATT BERRY STAPP EARP
(1848-1929)

Born: March 19, 1848 Monmout, Illinois.

Half-sister *Mariah Ann* died at the age of ten months.

Brothers *Newton*, *James* and *Virgil* joined
the Union Army on November 11, 1861.
Wyatt was too young at a mere 13 years of age.

January 10, 1870 aged 22 he married his first wife *Urilla Sutherland*
who tragically died the same year aged 21 during child birth.

In November of the same year he became CONSTABLE.

As a LAWMAN he was about to make HISTORY.

(continued p.101)

Brief script reading refresher…

Location line:

- **INT.** (interior) or **EXT.** (exterior)
- Locations are always listed from **LARGER** to **SMALLER**.
- **DAY** or **NIGHT** (other times like **DAWN** are unnecessary).
- **INT/EXT. A view from inside to outside. eg: Out of a window.**

Description:

- **Describe the environment in the present tense.**
- **Movement** and **actions** of actors.
- Possibly a point-of-view **POV** specific to one character.
- An actor's first appearance is **CAPITALIZED** with a **(micro description)**.

Character name:

- Always CAPITALIZED when followed by dialogue.
- Multiple names appearing on the same line means **actors talk together.**

Dialogue:

- **(parenthicals)** guidelines for the unobvious delivery of dialogue.
- **(…)** three dots **(ellipsis)** OR **(beat)** a **pause** the length of a drum beat.

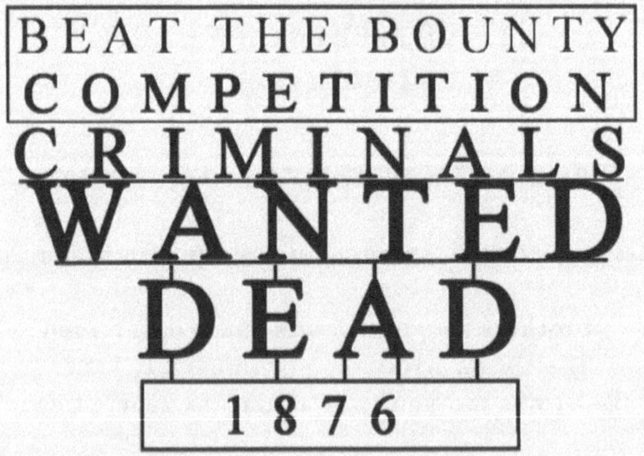

"Marin County, Beat the Bounty,
The wrong caliber need not apply."

- CHICAGO HERALD, 1876

FADE IN:

INT. PHILADELPHIA SUBURBS BEDROOM PRESENT DAY

WILD WEST diorama made up of action figures: DAYTONA (dirty bandit) sits on a DONKEY ahead of a line of UNION SOLDIERS.

YOUNG QUENTIN (artist) paints a Coast Miwok Indian warrior.

YOUNG QUENTIN (V.O.)
Every great Western starts with a flurry of action. The *Wild West* is such a vast topic, too broad to just start anywhere. What would my History teacher Miss. Prairie say?--

MS. PRAIRIE (V.O.)
--Focus Quentin, focus.

YOUNG QUENTIN (V.O.)
Yeah, she's good at that, focusing--

MS. PRAIRIE (V.O.)
--This presentation needs embellishing Quentin. Remember to try your best.

YOUNG QUENTIN (V.O.)
Father also says trying my best is what counts and to just *remember* where I came from.
(narrating)
One thing my family will *remember* is 1876, and today's story, which by modern standards surely is considered to be an urban legend, of a man, not written in any book you'll know of, but I will share the story with you all. One story told word of mouth to the tribes' children around a Lakota camp fire. Chief *Sitting Bull* himself spoke of a legendary sound; of *Spurs* carrying through the mountains which could make a newborn baby *smile* and a grown man *cry*. This is the legendary tale of the man who brought laughter to a nation. My great-great granddaddy, *Naked Spurs*.

MOTHER (O.S.)
Quentin! Dinner's on the table, it's getting cold!

YOUNG QUENTIN
O.K. ma'am.

Brush CHINKS into a pot of water.

MOTHER (O.S.)
Come and get it I won't tell you again!

YOUNG QUENTIN
(mumbles to himself)
What a Calamity.

Holds UNION COLONEL in the face of DAYTONA.

YOUNG QUENTIN AS UNION COLONEL
Go get your dinner Kid.

YOUNG QUENTIN AS DAYTONA
Your mouth's sure flapping. Who're you sayin' go get your dinner too? Who d'ya think you are?

YOUNG QUENTIN AS UNION COLONEL
Your momma.

Moves the DAYTONA figurine closer to UNION COLONEL.

YOUNG QUENTIN AS DAYTONA
Who you bad mouthin'? That mouth of yours'll sure land you in a shed load o' trouble.

Young-Quentin drops DAYTONA figurine. He notices a fleck of red paint on his thumb.

YOUNG QUENTIN AS DAYTONA
Colonel you no-good
(whispers)
Son of a bitch -- shot me.

DAYTONA topples over with throaty DEATH THROW noises.

YOUNG QUENTIN
(aloud)
One second mom!
(as Daytona)
I'll get you Colonel.
(as Union Colonel)
While you're down there kid kiss my...
(NAYS like an MULE)

MOTHER (O.S.)
You'll be eating the rear of a MULE if you don't come get it right-away.

YOUNG QUENTIN
(frantic)
I'm coming, don't give it to Bengi.

DOOR SLAMS: On the rear hangs an authentic WILD WEST *WANTED* POSTER franked with the words *BEAT THE BOUNTY - THE GREATEST MANHUNT IN HISTORY - CHICAGO HERALD, 1876.*

EXT. SAN MARIN HIGH SCHOOL DAY

Young-Quentin carries his DIORAMA and waddles towards the School with a PONY EXPRESS SATCHEL slung over his shoulder.

From car.

FATHER (O.S.)
Can you manage son?

YOUNG QUENTIN
Ok for a lift home tonight dad?

FATHER (O.S.)
Sure. Sock it to 'em kid!

YOUNG QUENTIN
Will do pops!

FATHER (O.S.)
Be sure to give Miss Prairie my regards.

INT. SAN MARIN HIGH SCHOOL HISTORY CLASS DAY

WILD WEST memorabilia adorns every wall.

FRONT OF CLASS Quentin adjusts the figures on his WILD WEST diorama.

MISS PRAIRIE sits at the back. She files through a pile of STUDENT ESSAYS which average a few pages each. Quentin's essay is a little light at a mere half a page in length.

CLOSE ON: CLASS REGISTER. A PEN TAPS next to a string of descending letters penciled after Quentin's name; "B-","C", "C-".

BACK TO SCENE

A seductive tone that every pubescent boy dreams of chirps up from the rear of the class...

MISS PRAIRIE

Eyes front. Quentin is telling us the tale of his great great grandfather. Everybody listen. Please start again Quentin. Go ahead.

He gulps.

YOUNG QUENTIN

The Wild West.

(beat)

The City Marshal's Office; a magnet for all criminals.

EXT. MARIN COUNTY HIGH STREET DAY, 1876

LABORERS ERECT A POLITICIAN'S PLATFORM.

Two JUVENILES aim a gun at a tin can.

ELSEWHERE AND WITHIN EARSHOT...

INT. MARIN COUNTY CITY MARSHAL'S OFFICE DAY

(O.S.) GUN SHOTS.

WYATT EARP (MARSHALL STAR) picks his teeth whilst his right hand DEPUTY paces to the window.

DEPUTY
It' a domestic.

QUENTIN (V.O.)
The prison of Marin County is already brimming with criminals. Town's getting restless; law-abiding citizens are now fighting amongst one another.

WYATT EARP
I've already put my feet up. I'm off duty.
(beat)
With all the GREAT GUNS idle any little puissant can get away with murder. This truly marks the end of an era. Trains bring in prospectors looking for a homestead, all shouting God bless America. Once upon a time, that would have been a hangman's platform out there, now it's a politician's. Some suit running for Major when he should be locking up those kids. Just where are their parents?

Onto feet.

WYATT EARP
I'm yet to see a political canon that aint all noise. Time's 'a' changing; one thing I can guarantee is I can still put a stop to this juvenile rot. I'm still a force to be reckoned with..

Puts on hat. Spurs chink towards the exit.

EXT. HIGH STREET PLATFORM DAY

Wyatt pins a poster *GUN BUYBACK PROGRAM - The devil makes work for Idle Hands, top prices for your pistola.*

SMELLY DOG, an unkempt Mexican pulls up in tarpaulin covered wagon. A rusty barreled pistol hangs from a rotten belt.

SMELLY DOG
Is that right? You give me good money for my Pistola?

WYATT
That's right. Even that rusty canon.

Smelly Dog lifts a tarpaulin on his wagon uncovering a cache of some TWENTY-PLUS army issue rifles.

SMELLY DOG
You like???

LATER THAT EVENING

INT. SALOON POKER TABLE DAY

Around sit four players. HAWK, a fat cigar smoking fur trader pushes a stack of chips into a pile. Smelly-dog puffs upon a cigar. The other two men are non-descript.

HAWK
That's everything. You either got it or you aint.

Cups the chips and pulls them towards himself.

SMELLY-DOG
That's a lot of money Mr. Hawk.

Smelly-dog reaches to his belt. Hawk draws his gun.

Smelly-dog carefully lifts the corner of his poncho to reveal a fist sized WAD of crisp cash in his holster. He pulls it like drawing a gun, dumping it onto the table.

SMELLY-DOG

That's everything Mr. Hawk. You know I don't count too good, but I can sure count on that being a lot of cash. Like you say... you either got it or you aint.

Hawk rocks back in his chair. His nostrils flare.

ELSEWHERE, IN THE LAND OF THE FREE...

INT. CHICAGO PRINTER'S BEDROOM DAY

PRINTER'S WIFE fastens her bustier around her pushed up half moons. DOC HOLIDAY (salubrious gent) gives her a hand.

PRINTER'S WIFE

I can hear him coming.

DOC

Your salacious comments tickle me.

PRINTER'S WIFE

Doc, my husband is coming.

INT./EXT. PRINTER'S UPPER BALCONY DAY

Doc throws a medical bag over the balcony into the street.

DOC

I lower myself to the level of insects by avoiding greater parasites?

EXT. PRINTER'S STOREFRONT DAY

Doc lands and deftly picks up his bag. A HERALD BOY turns with a "Where'd he come from?" expression.

HERALD BOY

Rag sir?

DOC
Pardon?

HERALD BOY
Gazette sir? A newspaper?

DOC
Why would I want to read about any one else's exploits?

HERALD BOY
Prestige sir.

DOC
You'd know about that?

HERALD BOY
Everybody loves to read about a hero sir. Deputies, outlaws. All good for business.

DOC
Quite an educated young chap aint we?

HERALD BOY
Thank you sir. My father owns this STORE.

DOC
Somewhat handy with the news aint you boy. I bet you know everything that goes on around here?

HERALD BOY
Some would pay to not be in the papers, if you know what I mean.

Newspaper-boy looks up to the balcony.

Doc swigs from a small bottle of liquor and takes two coins from his waistcoat breast pocket.

DOC
A bright little entrepreneur aint we?

HERALD BOY
Contains a Stagecoach coupon sir. Two for one.

DOC
Who am I going to be taking for a ride? Send my regards to your da'dy.

Takes newspaper, steadies his drunken stumble.

DOC
(drunkenly to himself)
Two for one. I pays for everything eventually.

INT. CHICAGO HERALD PHOTOGRAPHY ROOM DAY

WILD FRONTIER backdrop.

CALAMITY JANE, in "DAVY CROCKETT" attire poses with a long RIFLE; a raccoon tail completes her furry headgear.

The PHOTOGRAPHER crouches with FLASH.

PHOTOGRAPHER
Three -- two -- one. Hold that pose Calamity.

BRIGHT SULPHUROUS FLASH

With RIFLE aimed at the top of the backdrop. BANG!

Calamity shakes her headgear free. The backdrop falls, revealing a romanticized painting of WIGWAMS and TEE-PEES.

CALAMITY
And now... One for the boys.

Swinging her hips out... she sweeps back her hair and her purdy red lips blow smoke from the long smoldering barrel.

BRIGHT SULPHUROUS FLASH

CLOSE ON CHICAGO HERALD HEADLINE: "WILD FRONTIER" and the flirtatious image of CALAMITY. SUBTITLE: "NO MORE COWS at COW CITY"

BACK TO SCENE

MATCH CUT:

INT. HISTORY CLASS, SAN MARIN HIGH SCHOOL PRESENT DAY

Quentin holds the *CALAMITY JANE* CHICAGO HERALD article and taps his finger on the "NO MORE COWS AT COW CITY" article.

He turns and writes 'Fort Dodge / Cow City' on the board.

QUENTIN
Some of you may know, a great number of buffalo once roamed the plains around FORT DODGE. Prized for their hides the town flourished from this precious regional commodity and COW CITY was born.

Draws a line through FORT.

COW CITY became a victim of its own success; its commodity... the cows, slaughtered for their skins were to soon vanish from the plains.

Draws line through COW.

Without COWS, it reverted to its former name... DODGE. And so the infamous DODGE CITY name was forged.

Circles DODGE CITY.

Quentin picks up the PONY EXPRESS SATCHEL.

MATCH CUT:

INT. CITY MARSHAL'S OFFICE DAY, 1876

A MOUNTED MAIL OFFICER holds a PONY EXPRESS SATCHEL.

MOUNTED MAIL OFFICER
Pony express. MAIL!

SOON LATER...

Wyatt, letter in hand...

WYATT
There's only one farming solution to infectious cattle; you must slaughter the whole herd before it spreads like wildfire. The DEATH PENALTY for the MURDEROUS inmates of Marin County is to be made law by decree of Ulysses S. Grant, President of the United States February 1876.

INT. MARIN COUNTY PRISON COMMUNAL CELL DAY

Wagner's *RIDE OF THE VALKYRIES* scratches to a halt.

CHEWIE, MOUSE and SHADY stand side by side.

DAYTONA waves a thin cane.

DAYTONA
No no no. My granny would laugh at you. You're just not intimidating.

Pacing the line...

DAYTONA
Chewie, where's your tobacco?

Chewie opens his maw to show the BLACKNESS inside.

DAYTONA
When I say spit you spit.
(to Mouse)
You, *Mouse*. Too quiet! You must jangle.

Chewie attaches HORSE BRASS to Mouse's legs.

DAYTONA
Cool, and not too gay.

Daytona pulls Shady's SOMBRERO down to just above his eyes.

DAYTONA
Attitude. Give me more attitude.

Motioning to the OLDMAN holding a needle over a gramophone.

DAYTONA
Take it from the top.

The NEEDLE scratches and the MUSIC continues.

SERIES OF SHOTS A, B, C.

A) Chewie spits a nasty black glob which splats with a THWACK onto the floor.

B) Mouse stamps his foot to the sound of JANGLING metal.

C) Shady gives a steely gaze from beneath the brim of his SOMBRERO.

DAYTONA
Good, we are looking much tougher. Anyone seeing you will definitely know you are in my gang now.

EXT. MARIN COUNTY PRISON DAY

Prison graffiti reads: *You can book in but you'll never leave.* A SENTRY trudges across the gateway, rifle slung.

MOUNTED MAIL OFFICER rides in and throws down a mailbag.

INT. GOVERNOR'S OFFICE DAY

The GOVERNOR ponders over a letter from WYATT EARP. The

Mounted Mail Officer waits.

GOVERNOR
No one has ever escaped here, let alone ever been set free.

MAIL OFFICER
Hey, don't shoot the messenger.

GOVERNOR
Never before have I ever heard such cods-wallop.

The Governor lifts a quill from an inkwell.

GOVERNOR
You take this straight back to him.

MUCH LATER...

INT. CITY MARSHAL'S OFFICE DAY

Mounted Mail Officer waits: Wyatt reads Governor's letter.

WYATT
Beat the bounty?

MOUNTED MAIL OFFICER
The Governor's idea sir.

WYATT
Instead of executing them, have the WIDOWS execute justice.

MOUNTED MAIL OFFICER
Left it up to you to organize sir. Can I ask how you intend to carry out such a thing?

Wyatt steps up to the window.

WYATT
There may be justice in this world after-all. Hey, I'm getting all ROMANTIC. Maybe there is one last flurry for the great guns. (beat) Someone write my words down, this day could make me famous.

INT. PRISON BACKSTAGE DAY

Daytona, Chewie, Mouse and Shady stand behind a CURTAIN. From the other side comes the sound of many men talking.

DAYTONA

Shhh.

Daytona spins the barrel of his pistol and pops it into Mouse's holster.

DAYTONA

I think you *all* can take them. Ready? Give it all you got.

Very serious looks from Chewie, Mouse and Shady. They swish their poncho's aside and fingers twitch over their pistols.

DAYTONA

Nervous?

Each expresses various degrees of nervousness.

DAYTONA

I think we got 'em where we want them. Bring the house down.

O.S. SOUND of clunky communal hall PIANO.

CURTAIN RAISES

SERIES OF SHOTS A), B) and C)

A) Chewie takes a deep breath and spits a nasty black glob that splats with a THWACK onto the floor.

B) Mouse steps forward, stamps his foot to the rattle of polished metal.

C) Shady raises his head, gives a steely gaze from beneath the brim of his sombrero.

Thumbs hooked into belt; Chewie, Mouse and Shady line dance in front of a crowd of seated Union-soldiers who stamp their feet and clap along with the piano.

EXT. CHICAGO PRINTERS DAY

A HERALD BOY vends on a street corner.

PAPER BOY
Beat the Bounty. Read all about it.
Beat the Bounty sir. Gazette?

Doc hands over a coin.

PAPER BOY
Attracting the fastest guns in all
AMERICA to the *Wild West*.

DOC
Not all of them it aint.

CLOSE ON

A banner slung over a politician's platform. *Marin County, Beat the Bounty, the wrong caliber need not apply.*

DOC
The *Beat the Bounty* needs the right
caliber. A competition eh? Well I
do like a little challenge.

Pulls "TWO FOR ONE" STAGECOACH COUPON from his pocket.

EXT. UNION PACIFIC TRAIN STATION DAY

OLE TICKET VENDOR sits at window. A FLY BUZZES in his ear. He intermittently swats it.

SIGN 'TWO DOLLARS - MARIN COUNTY RETURN'

NO NAME (tall deft with gun slung) CHINKS across the platform. His reflection darkens the station window.

The Vendor looks up through the glass. No-name deftly passes a dollar coin across his knuckles.

OLE TICKET VENDOR
Will you be staying in Marin long?

A match strikes, No-name lights a SNUBBED CIGAR whilst still passing the coin knuckle to knuckle.

NO NAME
Depends how much of the lame herd they want shootin'.

OLE TICKET VENDOR
There's no herd in Marin County sir, just passing through eh?

NO NAME
Maybe.

OLE TICKET VENDOR
Two dollars return.

The FLY BUZZES louder in the Vendor's ear.

No-name's coin falls onto the counter -- seemingly spinning forever with a metallic SHING.

The Vendor gives a belly laugh.

No-name quick-draws. BANG!

Ole-ticket-vendor raises his hands.

OLE TICKET VENDOR
Don't kill me, please.

A crippled FLY twitches on its back near the spinning coin.

NO NAME
I either got it, or I aint.

OLE TICKET VENDOR
One way it is sir?

NO NAME
Is there any other way?

Ole-ticket-vendor shakes head and passes a SINGLE TICKET to *MARIN COUNTY*.

Leaning closer to the neat bullet hole in the glass...

NO NAME

Have a nice day.

The Ole-ticket-vendor claws back rickety finger and flicks the FLY off the counter.

INT. CHICAGO SIDEWALK DAY

Doc stands with a pyramid of suitcases. Calamity juggles a RIFLE and unravels the 'BEAT THE BOUNTY' poster.

DOC

Don't get me wrong, there's nothing wrong with ambition. Although you'll find aiming too high in a duel will get a lady killed.

CALAMITY

Who said I'm a lady?

A STAGECOACH pulls up. Doc throws suitcases up to the DRIVER. Calamity boards without Doc ever seeing.

DOC

How much convincing do you need? It's a contest attracting the fastest guns in the west. I'd liken the sport to swatting a swarm of insects. No doubt some with constitution will just soldier on into the night, but it'll be darn near a turkey shoot.

Doc looks to the empty sidewalk.

Calamity pokes her head from the carriage window.

CALAMITY

You coming or you just all talk?

EXT. STAGECOACH (MOVING) DAY

Rocking back and forth, Doc and Calamity sit either side of a small circular table. Each holds five cards.

Doc wears a black blazer, white shirt and black dickey-bow.

Calamity places a FULL HOUSE, three Jacks and two Queens on the table.

DOC

Bravo. Beginners luck.

Doc's places his cards face down.

DOC

Let me tell you about Dodge City, named after the fort, Fort Dodge. Nothing like Fort Worth. Ever been there?

CALAMITY

Never.

DOC

I'd make it worth your while. I'd take you right up the Chisholm Trail. I think you'd like that.

CALAMITY

Sounds like I may just swing your way.

Doc unbuttons his blazer.

DOC

In my haste it looks like you have the upper hand.

EXT. MARIN COUNTY STAGECOACH (MOVING) DAY

QUAKERS (HUSBAND and WIFE in classic bonnet).

O.S MEXICAN CRIMINALS HOLLER, bringing the stagecoach to a halt. PISTOLS of various barrel lengths poke into the carriage. One invites himself in.

He lifts the lady's petticoat with his gun barrel.

MEXICAN CRIMINAL
Now I don't want you to think that we're unreasonable men. You have one chance to get out, alive.

EXT. CHICAGO STAGECOACH (MOVING) DAY

Doc in white shirt and no dickey-bow; beneath the table ankle suspenders hold up his socks; he wears no trousers.

Calamity places a FULL HOUSE, three Jacks and two Queens on the table.

DOC
Play much Poker? You seem to be well versed in the *card art* of disrobing a man.

Doc deceives by placing his winning 'FOUR ACES' face down on the table and unbuttons his shirt.

DOC
Not long before we cross the Missouri.

CALAMITY
You mean the Mississippi.

DOC
The Mississippi? Darn. How slow can four wheels be?

CALAMITY
I could give you a hand in getting you right where you wanna be.

She pulls out a COUPON, TWO-FOR-ONE "UNION PACIFIC".

CALAMITY
A little HERALD BOY pulled some strings for me.

EXT. MOUNTAINS TRAIN (MOVING) DAY

A "UNION PACIFIC" STEAM LOCOMOTIVE CHUFFS up a steep climb.

INT. TRAIN PENTHOUSE CARRIAGE DAY

Stumpy RAILROAD TYCOON opens window and flicks cigar.

WIDOW-WHORE sits with all her petticoats flapping.

RAILROAD TYCOON
Too breezy for you baby?

WIDOW-WHORE
No, it's fine.

RAILROAD TYCOON
Cutting the landscape in all directions. Centuries in steel. Makes you kind-a-proud. You know how much steel it takes to lay a track from Kansas to Dodge City?

WIDOW-WHORE
Yes.
(stutters)
I mean, no.

RAILROAD TYCOON
Twenty-thousand tonnes. Know how much labor that takes?

WIDOW-WHORE
Many strong men.

RAILROAD TYCOON
A hell of a lot of strong men.

RAILROAD TYCOON
Have I told you this story?

WIDOW-WHORE
(lies)
No.

RAILROAD TYCOON
Show me an 'engineering feat' said the President and I showed him this. Whoever said a man can't move a mountain?

WIDOW-WHORE
Abraham Lincoln?

RAILROAD TYCOON
It's a metaphor darl', a metaphor for the resourceful folk that grafted every rail to the landscape. Even mountains they tunnel right through it like a frigging insect. See this huge tunnel ahead?

EXT. TUNNEL TRAIN (MOVING) DAY

Approaching the tunnel. Steam powered WHISTLE.

INT. DINING CARRIAGE DAY

O.S. WHISTLE.

Widow-whore files her nails. Tycoon rambles...

RAILROAD TYCOON

I'm brokering a lucrative contract with the Indians and the Army. Young man, a General supplying troops to whoever expands the frontier. I've heard he's hard to barter with. That boy will go far if he stays out of trouble.

(jogging memory)

Er...Custer, I'll remember that name.

A steam powered WHISTLE SCREAMS in the darkness.

EXT. MARIN COUNTY DAY

Wyatt addresses many wagons full of BOUNTY HUNTERS and homestead WIDOWS.

WYATT

You'll be hunting murderous 'horse thieves' and 'embezzlers'; not the traits of some of you virgin gunslingers. I'm not saying they're better shots than I, but I'm sure before the day is done, you'll have seen the whites of their eyes plenty, if you ever live to tell this tale. An unarmed man is an easy target if you can stomach it. One rule and I want you to stick to it. Who-ever reaches the Mexican border be he armed or unarmed is a FREE MAN... hence this competition BEAT THE BOUNTY, where a pardon *can* be earnt. The rest... Do unto others as they have done unto you.

EXT. PRISON DAY

Daytona reaches through the bars to a vat of *gruel*.

A PRISON DOLL with a noose around its neck hangs from the Gruel handle with a letter "NECKTIE PARTY" and a KEY.

Reading letter... Daytona spins the KEY.

DAYTONA
A cordial invite to a necktie party for all those reckoning on staying. This slop is your last supper and this KEY is for the front door.

A frenzy ensues. Prisoners leap for the KEY.

DAYTONA
STOP! STOP! You bloody THIEVES! Lets vote for who think they're a leader!

Crowd parts. A powerfully built bald BRUTE steps forth to oppose DAYTONA.

BRUTE tears up a piece of paper and hands them out.

BRUTE
This fight will be decided by a democratic vote.

BANG BANG

Brute falls over, two holes around his heart. Daytona stands holding a smoking DERRINGER.

DAYTONA
That's settled. The ballot swings in my favor. I'm leader.

He retraces his steps, taking back the slips of paper.

DAYTONA
I'll skip my poster campaign. I used to lead the best gang in all Mexico. They'd take a bullet for me. In fact they all took a bullet for me. Well actually, from me, but that's not my point; my point is they never complained, well not much. Squealed a little. "Don't kill me" in a weird high pitched voice which I found quite funny. See where this story's going? You wanna live, be in my gang. You dirty--

Counts the heads.

DAYTONA
--Way more than a *dozen*, more a *score*. A dirty score? That's not catchy. More of a Swarm. The dirty swarm? Yeah, the Swarm. And you're all my busy bees with a dirty sting in the tail.

DAYTONA
Any complaints?

SOON LATER...

Daytona masks the length of the two blades of grass in his hand.

DAYTONA
When those gates open it's going to be one turkey-shoot. Those who can run shall zig-zag and draw fire away from me. Those pulling the short straw will run first.

He looks around at the bruised scabby legs of most men.

DAYTONA
Can anyone run?

A FERRELL BOY, an INDIAN with brighter eyes that the rest catches his eyes.

DAYTONA
Hey you, Ferrell-boy. Do you think you can run?

He nods.

FERRELL INDIAN
I can outrun you.

Daytona's DERRINGER presses to his head, then turns it upon everyone else.

DAYTONA
Looks like we got ourselves a volunteer.
(relaxing)
Get him whatever he wants.

SERIES OF SHOTS

A dark corner contains a rusty pair of *spurs*.

A white foam spreads over the FERRELL INDIAN head to foot.

A dirty rag pulls away from the now clean spurs that shine like some new kind of holy relic.

Locks of hair fall to the floor.

Bald as a Coot he flexes his limbs like some naked Olympiad.

THE INFAMOUS BREAK OUT...

EXT. PRISON GATE DAY

VIGILANTES gather outside. Wagons hide a multitude of itchy trigger fingers. QUAKER WIDOWS point many rifles towards the gate.

(OVER) MUSIC ie: *2001 A Space Odyssey*

Gate CREAKS inwards.

One WIDOW raises her rifle to the ghostly sound of CHINKING SPURS which fades away.

SILENCE

A TUMBLEWEED passes.

CONTINUE MUSIC *2001 A Space Odyssey*

A lean INDIAN, naked as the day he was born runs as fast as a horse out through the gate, his every step ringing with the sound of chinking spurs…

Open mouthed she looks over her rifle, as do others who wait in ambush.

The bare bottom striding through their ranks towards the horizon mesmerizes the crowd.

MOMENTS LATER

ROAR from the criminal SWARM escaping the prison.

All turn to face the better part of a thousand men surging through the gate.

SPORADIC GUNFIRE and CRIES from FALLING MEN.

EXT. BLACK HILLS DAY

INDIANS amongst the towering sandstone buttes...

EAGLE EYES looks down from his vantage point. SITTING BULL (Sioux Chief) sits below with MANY TONGUES at his shoulder. LIGHT FOOT kneels at his side.

SITTING BULL
I am happy you came so soon.

LIGHT FOOT
I am happy brother.

SITTING BULL
Have you heard, the great white shark approaches?

LIGHT FOOT
Yes. Do they have horses?

Sitting-bull looks to Many-tongues who shakes his head.

LIGHT FOOT
No horses. We have ample time. Even our swiftest could not make Black Hills by nightfall.

EAGLE EYES hisses down from his vantage point.

Light-foot picks up his rifle and jogs to join him.

SOON LATER

Many-tongues and Light-foot look down through the buttes.

Sound of CHINKING SPURS

A lean INDIAN hurdles through the rocks near their position.

Light-foot raises his head above the rocks.

MANY TONGUES
Hey you!

The runner slows and looks up.

MANY TONGUES
Yeah you, yes you, naked man with spurs.

SOON LATER

All the Sioux huddle, arms folded with stern faces.

Many-tongues faces Sitting Bull, he raises his right hand covered in colorful war paint.

Sitting Bull nods.

O.S. SOUND of SLAP-SLAP upon bare flesh.

LEAN INDIAN "NAKED SPURS"
Ahrh! Wahhrr!

O.S. SOUND of CHINKING SPURS running away.

Sitting Bull, arms folded, stands stern faced.

Naked Spurs CHINKS towards the horizon with a colorful handprint on each buttock.

Sitting Bull unfolds his arms and slaps his thigh...

...crumples over with belly aching laughter...

...Standing he points in the direction *Naked Spurs* ran and

wipes a tear from his eye then continues to laugh.

EXT. LOG CABIN DAY

Daytona and the Swarm watch from the tree-line.

DAYTONA
It's as good a place as any to hole up. But there aint gonna be enough room for all, better draw straws.

They look at him suspiciously.

DAYTONA
I promise to not shoot no-one.

Loads his Derringer.

DAYTONA
(to himself)
That's a double-negative if you're wondering. I'm a Mexican.

INT. LOG CABIN NIGHT

Around a table stand SEVEN of the Swarm: THOUGHTLESS BRAWLER, UNSHAVEN TRAMP, TOOTHLESS COOT, OPIUM ADDICT, BEARDED BUFFOON, FAT CATTLEMAN and Daytona. In a box on the table lay an apple-pie cut into six pieces.

Daytona looks amongst them.

DAYTONA
Only six pieces of pie between the seven of us, and I'm guessing every dwarf's hungry? Am I right?

THOUGHTLESS BRAWLER
What if someone is *really* hungry?

TOOTHLESS COOT
(lisps)
Has a big mouth or wants two slices?

Unshaven-tramp looks to the Fat-cattleman.

UNSHAVEN TRAMP
Or has a bigger belly?

DAYTONA
I believe in us all each having a slice. But like I said. We're *one* too many.

Daytona tips the bullets out of his Derringer 'til only one remains. He closes the gun and spins the chamber.

DAYTONA
No time to mess about, no funny business, I'm just going clockwise.

Cocking the hammer, he aims at everyone in turn, left to right.

Thoughtless-brawler frowns and steps back from the table.

CLICK

DAYTONA
That would have been way too easy.

Daytona points to Unshaven-tramp's face, his smile drops.

CLICK

Toothless-coot gurns a gummy grin and closes his eyes.

CLICK

Opium-addict opens his jacket showing a tattooed target on his belly. Daytona points at the bulls-eye.

CLICK

Bearded-buffoon twists the dry ends of his ginger beard.

CLICK

Fat-cattleman breaks from the table and runs for the door.

BANG

Fat-cattleman falls - hand to his back.

Toothless-coot laughs outrageously.

DAYTONA
Did you not like him? What's so funny?

TOOTHLESS COOT
I don't like apple pie.

DAYTONA
Well what a predicament, now we have a slice too many.

Daytona points the gun at Toothless-coot and pulls the trigger five times causing him to wince with every CLICK.

DAYTONA
Now that's funny. You aint a very nice person, but I like you! Anyone else not like apple pie?

Thoughtless-Brawler reverses a chair and sits, broad smile.

THOUGHTLESS BRAWLER
Isn't APPLE PIE just dandy!?

DAYTONA
You wanna die over a stale crust? I'm sure who-ever cut it will be back soon. On principal, no one touches the pie, got it? Now get your heads down, we gotta lot of running to do in the morning.

NEXT DAY...

EXT. SHALLOW RIVER DAY

Thirsty Swarm members rush to drink at the water's edge.

One spots a HORSE grazing on the opposing bank.

RENEGADE CAVALRY OFFICER
A horse!?

MEXICAN

A horse!

The rush escalates into a whitewater stampede.

The Swarm create the biggest white-water fistfight in history. A melee, each trying to be the first to the horse.

Lots of head dunking, garroting and four knuckle sandwiches.

The RENEGADE CAVALRY OFFICER is first over and waves to the Mexicans from the back of his new mount.

RENEGADE CAVALRY OFFICER

Hasta luego! So long suckers!

He trots away up the embankment.

At the summit he pauses then gallops upstream.

SOON LATER

Mexicans continue to yell at the Renegade-cavalry-officer as they reach the opposing riverbank.

POV RISING OVER THE EMBANKMENT

Reaching the summit they HOLLER with joy and run from view.

Every criminal HOLLERS all the way towards a RANCH full of horses.

30 MINUTES LATER...

EXT. QUIET RANCH DAY

A broken fence destroys the aesthetics of this homestead.

Daytona swipes dust from his boots.

A DUTIFUL WIFE pulls a small pale of water from a WELL. A large BUCKET nearby lay broken.

DAYTONA

Hey you! Yeah you.

A HUMBLE HUSBAND and TWINKLE-EYED SON step out of the shadowy dwelling.

DAYTONA
Fresh water, and a ride.

HUMBLE HOMESTEADER
There *are* no horses left mister.
I'm lucky they left my plough.

DAYTONA
No bull?

Daytona strikes a match and lights a cigar.

DAYTONA
Still living aint yah, looks like
you got off lightly.

O.S. WHINNEY from a DONKEY.

CLICK of Derringer at his hip.

INT/EXT. RICKETY BARN DAY

At gunpoint the Humble-husband opens the door. His Twinkle-eyed-son clings to his Dutiful-wife's leg.

CLICK of Daytona's pistol at the Humble-Husband's ear.

DAYTONA
Beggars can't be choosers. He'll
do.

EXT. RICKETY BARN DAY

Daytona secures the barn by padlocking it shut.

Walking the DONKEY to the WELL he offers it a palm of water and swigs from a half-full PALE himself. A key PLOPS down onto the water's surface.

DAYTONA
I have plans for us, Donkey. We'll go along way together: Mexico.

Chambers bullets, spins it with multiple CLICKS.

The Donkey's ears remain still.

DAYTONA
Hmmm?

BOOM at his ear! The Donkey remains still.

DAYTONA
What's a deaf donkey to me? Could be quite an obedient steed. Don't worry Donkey I won't have a bad word said about you. Guess we better be going.

HOURS LATER

EXT. OPEN PLAIN DAY

A PEACE LOVING QUAKER and WIFE ride a two-wheeled carriage along a dirt track. They stop at a Donkey tethered to a tree. Daytona buttons his fly then raises his gun.

DAYTONA
Go for your gun.

PEACE LOVING QUAKER
Guns - are the weapons of Sinners.

DAYTONA
Do you not think they represent free speech? They certainly don't separate Saints from Sinners.

Lowers hammer on pistol, taps temple with tip of barrel.

DAYTONA
I'm sure we theologians can think of something that can settle this theological dichotomy?

SOON LATER

WIFE SCREAMS

Her husband spins, dragged in the dirt behind the carriage.

His tearful Wife runs to his aid when he stops.

DAYTONA
Back to my point. You were saying
I'm a Sinner?

Daytona toys with her husband at the end of his barrel.

DAYTONA
You may be right, you may walk the
higher moral ground, but don't it
sting like a bitch?

Her husband flinches when she touches him.

He holsters his firearm and she gives Daytona dagger-eyes.

DAYTONA
Hey, I didn't shoot no-one.
(rhetorical)
Aint I a Saint.

EXT. MARIN COUNTY BLACKSMITH DAY

BLACKSMITH (muscular bronze) addresses CUSTOMER.

CUSTOMER
My horse has kicked a shoe.

No-name trots to the post, dismounts and tethers it.

NO NAME
My horse has *no* shoes; and I have a
bigger gun. I'll be back by noon
for a fully shoed horse.
(tips hat)
Gentlemen.

INT. ZIMMERMANN'S HARDWARE DAY

MONOCLE (elderly proprietor) with trademark eyewear; hands Mouse a pair of custom boots. Shady guards the door.

MONOCLE
Ah, the bespoke boots.

He goes out back.

SHADY
Did yaw do what I said?

Monocle returns and shows him the soles.

MONOCLE
'R' for RIGHT and 'L' for LEFT just like you said.

SHADY
Saying' my brother's dumb?

MONOCLE
Only one extra dollar. No one will ever notice.

SHADY
You chargin' him for being dumb?

Monocle stutters nervously.

MONOCLE
No-no. I just said a dollar extra. Call it fifty cents eh? I'm sure you boys are returning customers.

SHADY
Put it on the tab.

MONOCLE
No credit sir. I don't keep tabs.

SHADY
You sayin' we're not good for it?

MONOCLE
Now, I d-didn't say that.

SHADY
You sayin' my brother aint got the brains to remember twenty-five cents?

MONOCLE
I'll open up a tab immediately so w-we don't forget the outstanding balance of fifty cents.

SHADY
You have a nice day now you hear. Just how you think we're to make a profit with you all keepin' ripping us off?

Monocle nods, gives a compromising wave.

Door chime JINGLES. Enter a HAIRY PROSPECTOR who swaggers to a pair of scales on the counter. The scales TINK with gold nuggets.

Monocle brings a tray of weights to the scales.

MONOCLE
That's...

Counter-balances the scales.

MONOCLE
...forty dollars.

TINK of huge nugget upon the pan.

MONOCLE
Forty-five dollars.

Peels a few bills from a roll of cash.

MONOCLE
Take it or leave it.

The Hairy prospector slams a hand on the dollar bills.

HAIRY PROSPECTOR
In Chicago Black Hill gold get me ninety!

MONOCLE
This aint Chicago.

Door chime TINKLES on his way out.

Monocle picks up the weights and goes out-back.

Door chime TINKLES.

SPURS CHINK to the counter.

TINK TINK TINK upon the scales.

Monocle returns with the tray of weights. Places a weight on the scale and looks up to see three bloody gold teeth in the pan.

MONOCLE
Fifteen dollars.

CLICK CLICK of Daytona's pistol hammer drawing back.

MONOCLE
Not enough?

Daytona's pistol barrel TINKS against the proprietor's monocle.

MONOCLE
Twenty dollars?

Again, TINK TINK upon his monocle.

MONOCLE
Thirty dollars?

DAYTONA
A fair price to pay wouldn't you say?

Monocle nods.

DAYTONA
I knew you'd see sense. That's what they pay in Chicago.

MONOCLE
So I hear.

Daytona folds the money on the counter with one hand.

DAYTONA
If a respectable friend were ever to stay in a town such as this, where would you say is a fair place?

MONOCLE
The 'Last Chance Inn'.

DAYTONA
You ever stay there?

Monocle nods, then shakes his head. His monocle falls off into the tray of gold teeth.

DAYTONA
I like you. I think you're a fair man, I may be sending some more business your way.

Pats his pocket.

Another bloody tooth lands in the pan.

DAYTONA
On the house.
(double-takes)
Second thought. Start me a tab.

O.S. GUNSHOTS FROM OUTSIDE

DAYTONA
I hate anyone owing me anything.

Daytona picks up a hat and leaves by the back door.

DAYTONA
Call it even.

EXT. STREET NIGHT

DOC zigzags bullets in a drunken stupor; A ROTUND-BANDIT laughs, another with SHORT-LEGS packs two pistols.

DOC
I smell something brewing, or do you suffer problem body areas?

Looks Short-legs up and down.

DOC
Short legs, pregnant, shall I go on?

Short-legs unbuckles both his pistols.

DOC
I may be way off the trail with my assessment of your candor. You brothers may be just 'style' challenged heathens. I'm not sure.

Rotund-bandit draws a pistol from his shoulder holster.

DOC
Ah that's a mighty rusty piece you have there fatso, care to slip it back into your Otter's pocket?

Doc unbuttons his waistcoat, it falls down into one hand.

DOC
I'm unarmed gentlemen, see. Though I am bare-knuckle champion of the 'Chicago all boys club' if you fancy a round or three.

Swings waistcoat over shoulder and disarmingly walks away.

DOC (O.S.)
Look at those stars. Look, the Great Bear. Darn, that one looks like me sucking on both your momma's titties.

Both men run; turning the corner Doc is nowhere to be seen.

EXT. QUIET RANCH DUSK

A GINGER FARM GIRL cocks a RIFLE in Calamity's direction.

GINGER FARM GIRL
Hands up.

CALAMITY
Aint you a little young to be out
little lady?

GINGER FARM GIRL
I'm old enough.

CALAMITY
Yeah sure? You look like you're
about to cry.

GINGER FARM GIRL
No I aint.

Calamity draws. BANG!

Legs buckling she hits the floor, blood pours from her knee.

GINGER FARM GIRL
(wincing, crying)
You shot me.

Sobs.

CALAMITY
Dumb kid. I knew you were gonna
cry. Here, I'm sorry.

Calamity covers the wound with a handkerchief.

CALAMITY
Next time leave the fighting to the
big girls. I'm sorry. You'll mend.
Where's a doctor when you need one?

GINGER FARM GIRL
Father's a doctor. He's trapped in
the barn.

EXT. CAMPFIRE NIGHT

Wyatt and a POSSE sleep.

SCREAM from OLDHAND (venerable cowboy)

OLDHAND
ARGH! I'm bit.

Wyatt kicks the brush besides his bedding.

There's a RATTLE sound.

WYATT
Woh... it's a Rattler all right.

OLDHAND
I'm gonna die.

Wyatt trips the crazed Oldhand to the floor. Two red dots puncture the man's index finger. Wyatt raises a machete.

OLDHAND
I'm a craftsman. Not the hand!

WYATT
Bite down on this.

A short thick stick now plugs the crazed man's mouth.

Wyatt raises the machete.

WYATT
Tuck in any pinkies you wanna keep.

Wyatt CHOPS down firmly.

OLDHAND
Mwaaargh!

LATER

Oldhand hand bandaged within a sling sits by a crackling fire.

WYATT
Just what exactly were you shuffling in your blanket that looked just like a mouse? You were lucky to have only lost your finger.

INT. HOTEL BEDROOM NIGHT

Doc, waistcoat in hand. A naked GAY BANDIT points a pistol.

GAY BANDIT
Take your pants and boots off slowly.

DOC
You're smooth. Aint one for foreplay are we?

Doc undoes his belt.

DOC
Not even a nightcap?

LATER

Doc sits naked, both hands cover his scrotum. The Gay-bandit fits Doc's clothes perfectly.

DOC
Now if I knew that was your original intention I have a spare set in my closet.

Doc opens the closet and shows identical clothes.

INT/EXT. HOTEL WINDOW DAY

Doc sees the Rotund bandit and his Short-legs brother tie up their horses.

DOC
Oh, just my luck.

INT. HOTEL CLOSET DAY

The Gay-bandit smiles. A pair of PISTOLS with IVORY handles rest upon a BOWLER. Doc deflates.

DOC
Not the hat, it's custom-made.
Pistols too; everyone knows they're
mine, they're unique. Come-awn!?#

MOMENTS LATER

EXT. STREET DAY

The Gay-bandit tips Doc's BOWLER hat and crosses the street away from Calamity and a hobbling Ginger-girl.

CALAMITY
Doc?

Rotund-bandit and Short-legs exchange looks, they draw and shoot him... BANG-BANG ...in the back.

CALAMITY (O.S.)
DOC!

Both men mount their horses and take flight.

Calamity rushes to the corpse.

CALAMITY
Doc? Doc!
(to street)
Someone get a doctor!

From over her shoulder...

DOC
I hear a reputable doctor stays at
this abode. Is there a problem?

Without looking at the good Samaritan...

CALAMITY
I need a doctor urgently.

A HERALD REPORTER (20's) runs to the body.

DOC (O.S.)
He's nothing but a darn-robber. I'd be more careful in choosing your friends missy.

Calamity turns, sees a naked Doc with hands on his scrotum.

DOC
Could you please be a lady and pass me my hat?

CALAMITY
Why you!?

Calamity storms off across the street.

DOC
That's gratitude for yah. This town's full of nothing more than robbers and rude people.

HERALD REPORTER
I need a statement.
(to Doc)
You sir.

Doc paces to the hotel lobby with reporter in tow.

DOC
Yes, I knew him, quite well. John 'Doc' Holliday, a drunkard, a gun fighter. A hell of a guy.

REPORTER
And you are? Your name sir?

DOC
My wife thinks I'm peddling wares in Chicago. Keep my name out the papers sonny and I'll give you a story: Wyatt Earp was once fined a dollar for assaulting a prostitute. He was onto a good thing 'cause Doc said she charged him at least two.

INT. SALOON BAR NIGHT

Daytona downs a *shot* of whiskey. BARTENDER with his fingers in the SHOT glass lifts it then wipes the counter.

Wyatt rushes in.

WYATT
A ranch has been rustled. A horde of criminals calling themselves *The Swarm* have made off with all the livestock.

BARTENDER
You going after them? It's late.

WYATT
Little chance waiting here for them.

Wyatt gives Daytona a lingering look so he tips his hat and returns a smile.

Wyatt exits.

BARTENDER
Hey stranger, you ever heard of a gang called the *Swarm* led by a *greasy dago* called Daytona?

DAYTONA
Why who's asking?

BARTENDER
Someone came 'round, shouting his mouth off. Said he was looking for Daytona.

DAYTONA
Are there many people looking for this Daytona?

BARTENDER
This one was different; he said he was going to kill Daytona.

DAYTONA
This man, did he have a name?

BARTENDER
Lucky criminal? Lucky thief?

DAYTONA
Lucky Crook?

BARTENDER
Yeah that's it. You know him?

DAYTONA
Did he say where he was staying?

He draws a pistol in the Bartender's face.

BARTENDER
Across the street.

DAYTONA
There's a thousand-and-one ways to kill a man. This is just six of them.

Downs *shot* of whiskey.

DAYTONA
If I ever see this Daytona, I'll make sure to pass on your message.

EXT. WILDERNESS TRAIL DAY

Wyatt prowls the tree-line right of the trail.

Mouse and Shady prowl to the left. Chewie armed with a double barrel shotgun hasn't seen them yet.

SHADY
Shhh...it's Chewie and he's armed.

Shady raises a pistol and aims for his torso.

Chewie's head appears at the end of his sights.

SHADY
Chew on this.

BANG

Mouse runs towards the downed shotgun.

MOUSE
Finders keepers.

Wyatt raises his gun to the rattle of Mouse's HORSE BRASS.

SHADY
Mouse you dumb mother.

Mouse appears at the end of Wyatt's barrel.

BANG. Mouse falls.

WYATT
Noisy son of a--

--Twigs snap on Wyatt's flank.

Shady breaks through the undergrowth just as Wyatt raises Chewie's shotgun.

BOOM.

Shady flies back; the sole of his boot showing an "R".

WYATT
"R"-sole.

EXT. DESERT DAY

UNION SOLDIERS rest. A UNION GENERAL talks to a Herald-reporter.

HERALD REPORTER
I'm investigating a death. What unit are you from?

UNION GENERAL
The Army of *The Tennessee,* not to be confused with Army of Tennessee or The Army of West Tennessee. Which became the Army of Mississippi which then merged with our Army of The Tennessee under Major General Ulysses S. Grant?

HERALD REPORTER
So you're in the Army of Tennessee?

UNION GENERAL
No. *The Tennessee* sir.

HERALD REPORTER
The Army of *The Tennessee*?

UNION GENERAL
Yes.

HERALD REPORTER
Not West Tennessee?

UNION GENERAL
That's right.

HERALD REPORTER
Under Ulysses S. Grant?

UNION GENERAL
The very man himself.

The Union-general walks off. The Herald-reporter turns to a UNION SOLDIER.

HERALD REPORTER
Who died?

UNION SOLDIER
Not sure. Some soldier, if that's of any help. From the Mississippi. Or the Missouri, wasn't quite listening? I hear its good fishing up that way.

FLASHBACK: INT. BLACKSMITH'S DAY

Daytona lifts a GLOWING HORSESHOE from the fire.

LUCKY CROOK cowers.

DAYTONA
So what'll it be? An eye for an eye? Honor among thieves? Huh?

LUCKY CROOK
No!

DAYTONA
Feeling lucky?

Daytona rubs chin. CLICKS fingers and TWO BANDITS hold LUCKY CROOK by the arms.

DAYTONA
With so many illiterate criminal friends, I have to rely on a man's word. I'm a fair man. But one thing I hate most; is a lazy rustler who leaves too many loose ends, fails to cross the "I"s and dot the "T"s.

Daytona thrusts a GLOWING HORSESHOE into Lucky-crook's face.

Shrill SCREAM.

INT. CRIPPLE CREEK BAR POKER TABLE DAY

Hundred dollar bills and *IOU* notes show the importance of the pot upon the poker table. At the table sit HAWK (a fat cigar smoking fur trader), DEAD EYES (a blue-eyed cold killer), WHITE MAN APACHE (a wandering scout of duel ethnicity) and Lucky-crook (with a hat obscuring his face).

Hawk chews a cigar and fans a winning hand the breadth of his smile.

HAWK
Full house gentlemen.

Dead-eyes remains motionless. White-man-apache turns over losing cards.

Lucky-crook throws his cards and stands.

LUCKY CROOK

How could a low-life Vulture like you come to be known as Hawk?

HAWK

Same reason a loser like you could be called Lucky Crook. Irony I guess.

Hawk tosses him a CHIP.

HAWK

Here, sit down, we don't want any bad blood between us.

(to White-man-apache)

No offense.

(to Lucky-crook)

Come-awn sit down. Rustle up another hand.

LUCKY CROOK

Screw you.

Lucky-crook pulls his hat down over his face and leaves.

Hawk gathers the cards and receives a stern look from White-man-apache.

HAWK

Something I said?

Hawk shuffles the deck.

HAWK

Well are you in or not?

Deals out another hand.

HAWK

Wigwams don't come cheap.

INT/EXT. HOTEL BEDROOM WINDOW DAY

Daytona tracks Calamity with his pistol, she strides into the centre of the street.

INT. HOTEL BEDROOM WINDOW DAY

FLOORBOARD CREAKS.

Daytona looks to the door. A shadow moves beneath.

DAYTONA
The Queen's gambit?

Daytona cocks his pistol.

EXT. HOTEL DAY

Calamity looks around the street.

INT. HOTEL 1st FLOOR LANDING DAY

Lucky-crook holds a double barreled shotgun; he rocks his foot back onto its heel with a SQUEAK.

Daytona's shadow passes under the door of one bedroom.

LUCKY CROOK
Peek-a-boo.

The twin barrels hover at the keyhole.

BOOM! The door swings inwards with a huge bite taken out.

And he makes a quick CLICK-CLICK reload crossing over the threshold.

INT. HOTEL BEDROOM DAY

SCUFF from within the closet, its door remains open an inch.

Lucky-crook's barrel rises to the dark crack. He eases the door open with an EERIE CREAK.

Daytona stands behind the main bedroom door, his pistol points through the bite-sized hole.

BANG BANG

Lucky-crook falls into the wardrobe.

DAYTONA
Guess you're not such a lucky crook after-all. Well ya found me.

BANG.

Daytona closes the wardrobe door on a man with a horse-shoe brand on his face and a bullet hole in his forehead.

EXT. SALOON DAY

Doc downs a whiskey, he sees Wyatt's reflection in the bar mirror. A CUSTOMER stands at Doc's elbow.

WYATT
I once thought I'd lost my morals. And you know what? I had. But now that I have them back I know right from wrong. If we fell out I'd shoot your sorry ass in the back.

DOC
(to Wyatt's reflection)
I'd never forgive you if you do.
(beat)
Since when does being an embezzling cattle rustler make anyone a Marshal? They still blind to your many wrong doings?

WYATT
Your mother thinks I'm an outstanding citizen.

DOC
You bastard.

WYATT
Draw and I'll drop you quicker than you lost your will to be a decent human being.

CUSTOMERS at the bar move away from Doc. Doc turns to face Wyatt. Both attempt to out stare each other.

They laugh like big kids and hug like good old friends, ending their charade.

WYATT
Doc you son of a bitch.

DOC
No need to get personal. Did I mention that I more than kissed both your sisters?

WYATT
Brothers?

DOC
Oh dear, that must have been one hell of a night, I must have had one too many.

WYATT
(to Bartender)
A bottle of your finest BOURBON for this gentleman. Let's celebrate.

EXT. STREET DAY

A bunch of *The Swarm* approach, if a tooth aint gold it's black or missing.

A SCHOOLMA'AM holds a handkerchief to her nose.

LADY
You smelly swine.

DAYTONA
Hey, I hope you're not stereotyping me. I'm a nice guy. You'll give me a complex.

His henchmen laugh.

DAYTONA
(to men)
Hey, she hurt my feelings.

Further laughter.

FLASHBACK: EXT. THEATER DAY

A PASTE MAN pastes a *ROMEO AND JULIET* poster onto a billboard. The POSTER depicts a man and woman in Italian *period* costume. A HERALD REPORTER sets up his tripod.

CHINK of spurs; it's only Daytona and the SWARM (Chewie and Mouse, Shady, Toothless-coot and KILLJOY (a tobacco-sucking ruffian).

The Paste-man's brush shakes.

DAYTONA
We interrupting anything?

HERALD REPORTER
No. It's Shakespeare.

Killjoy stares at him.

KILLJOY
Rome-O and Juli-et?

He spits black tobacco into the Paste-man's bucket.

DAYTONA
No you idiot. Romeo and Juliet.

The Swarm laugh.

DAYTONA
If my pistola be the fruit of love,
your sister Killjoy would dance on!
Yeah, I love that dat-opera.

He fires his pistol at the Paste-man's feet causing him to dance.

The Swarm also fire bullets at the floor and holler. A bullet strikes the Paste man's foot causing him to fall.

SILENCE

Daytona walks up the line of men, Killjoy's Sombrero tilts lower than the others.

DAYTONA
You not like what I say about your
sister? Did I say shoot him?

Daytona knocks Killjoy's sombrero off.

DAYTONA
Can't you see, you just spoilt our
fun? What a killjoy.

Points up the High Street.

DAYTONA
Run. That way.

Daytona turns his back on Killjoy. Gun in hand he spins his six barrels and blindly points pistol over his own shoulder.

DAYTONA
Get running.

POV over his shoulder, Killjoy runs up the street.

DAYTONA
Chewie, give me some help here.

Chewie looks over Daytona's shoulder.

CHEWIE
Up, down a bit. Left, left. Hold it.

BANG! A bullet bounces in the dirt at Killjoy's feet.

Daytona turns to see the dirt settle.

DAYTONA
Tut-tut. Come back. Game over! I let you live.
(to Swarm)
Shall I let him live?

CHEWIE	MOUSE	SHADY	TOOTHLESS COOT
(tilts head)	(shakes head)	(nods)	(rocks hand)

Daytona offers his hand to Killjoy.

Killjoy reaches out with a flat HAND like the children's game 'Paper, Scissors, Stone'.

Daytona's FINGERs are FORKED like a pair of scissors.

BANG

DAYTONA
SCISSORS always beats PAPER.

Killjoy falls.

DAYTONA
What? Everybody knows scissors beats paper. I'd let him live if he would of won. Honest. Cross my heart.

The Swarm remain shocked.

DAYTONA
You no believe me?
(to Paste-man)
You believe? Sorry about foot.
(glances at poster)
Life's one big tragedy.

Daytona leads the Swarm across the street.

DAYTONA
Chewie, remind me to take *your* sister to see Romeo and Juliet.

Chewie gives a stern look.

DAYTONA
What, you think she'll not like it? Women love to be serenaded.

INT. BARBERS DAY

The BARBER tentatively shaves up to Doc's sideburns.

CLICK of Doc's pistol in his groin.

DOC
That's close enough.

BARBER
I'll not take anything more than I aught to.

DOC
I'm just guaranteeing it. Let me tell you about my friend Wyatt Earp and a little band we created called the 'Peace Commission'.

MUCH LATER

INT. MASSAGE PARLOR DAY

A MASSEUSE gives Doc a *rosewater* massage.

DOC
Well that's the hogwash I told the Barber next door. Still, style never goes out of fashion. Neither does the smell of an endearing rose.

INT. PHOTOSHOP DAY

PHOTOGRAPHER and tripod, MISSY (wife-assistant) stands at his side. Doc sits in front of a theatrical backdrop. He holds his chin and leans closer, smiling to Missy.

DOC
Close enough for ya?

The Photographer disappears under a blanket.

A sulphurous FLASH causes stars to twinkle in Doc's eyes.

DOC
Too close?

Doc rubs his eyes then his chin.

Photographer hands plate to his wife and slides another plate into the camera.

DOC
Do try to develop that one, twas a real good shave; be a shame not to capture it for prosperity.

MISSY
I'll process this plate right away Mr. Holliday.

PHOTOGRAPHER
Another?

DOC
Take your time Missy, quality is worth waiting for.

Missy gives a demure smile.

DOC
Aint she just flirty? Sure, shoot away my good man.

FLASH: More stars in the eyes.

EXT. STREET ZIMMERMANN'S HARDWARE STORE DAY

Doc bites the tip of his cigar.

Calamity smells the air.

CALAMITY
(in Doc's accent)
Do I detect the fragrance of an endearing rose?

Doc turns.

Calamity's face lights up.

DOC
I do declare myself as a new age metro sexual, Calamity.

CALAMITY
Nice to see you *alive* and *kicking.*

DOC
I don't wish to be rude with my hasty departure Missy but a prior engagement draws me away from your alluring presence. Forgive me for excluding myself from your company.

CALAMITY
Yeah, see you 'round.

Doc throws her a HOTEL KEY.

DOC
Calamity you certainly redefine the strength of a woman in both attire and aroma. Smell you later baby.

Calamity smells her own armpit.

CALAMITY
How rude.

Then looks at the LAST CHANCE SALOON key fob in her hand.

EXT/INT. LAST CHANCE SALOON 1st FLOOR DAY

POV through Doc's RIFLE SCOPE through a window across the street.

He spies the bare flesh of Calamity preparing to bathe.

DOC (O.S.)
Oh my, I have surely set a new benchmark for deviousness.

In front of a CHEVAL mirror she disrobes, pantaloons first.

DOC (O.S.)
Least she's not lost her mother's rosy cheeks. What a woman.

A PROWLER with a raised CANDLESTICK reflects in her CHEVAL mirror. Doc lowers his aim to a shiny waist buckle.

P.O.V. of Prowler through Doc's RIFLE SCOPE.

DOC
I declare, a *prowler* in the bedroom with a candlestick.

CLICK-CLICK of rifle cocking then BANG!

INT. 1st FLOOR LAST CHANCE SALOON DAY

The WINDOW SMASHES.

Calamity SCREAMS.

A candlestick CLUNKS to the floor. Falling to his knees the Prowler lay bent over with his pants round his ankles.

INT/EXT. LAST CHANCE SALOON 1st FLOOR WINDOW DAY

Across the street she sees Doc tips his hat and withdraw his rifle through his window.

INT/EXT. HOTEL 1st FLOOR BEDROOM DAY

Calamity shuts her curtain.

DOC
Much obliged ma'am. Anytime.

EXT. STREET DAY

SHILLING (a cold calculated killer) trails Wyatt up the street.

Daytona watches the whole from over his own gun sights.

BANG. Wyatt falls.

Daytona watches Shilling open his smoking gun.

CLOSE ON: Shilling's BARREL SPINS SLOWLY, of the five bullets that fall out each has a name etched on it.

BACK TO SCENE

DAYTONA
(uncocks pistol)
Hmm.
(to himself)
Mr. Shilling, what an intriguing game you play.

INT. DOCTOR'S OFFICE DAY

Upon the wall hangs a TOMAHAWK AXE and an assortment of bloodstained ARROWHEADS and BENT BULLETS.

WINCING of Wyatt biting down upon a splint. A sweaty Doc rummages around his wound with a pair of scissors.

DOC
Darn it.

WYATT
Easy.

Locates bullet.

DOC
Here she is.

The bullet TINKS into a pan.

Wyatt pants hard.

Doc grabs a bottle of whiskey and takes a swig himself.

WYATT
Remind me, never to ask you for a tattoo.

DOC
Sorry, helps me deal with stress.

Offers the bottle to Wyatt who finishes the bottle.

Doc wipes the bullet on Wyatt's bloodstained shirt and scrutinizes it closely.

DOC
Kind of personal.

"WIATT" is inscribed on the bullet.

WYATT
It's spelt wrong.

DOC
How fortuitous, a gift from an illiterate well-wisher.

WYATT
I don't believe in "fate". Man makes his own luck and I am going to spell it out to him, one bullet at a time. Doc hand me my pistol.

Doc gives Wyatt back his pistol.

DOC
You're the "Law of the land", that's 12 bullets.

Wyatt catches Doc's pistol and slides it into the rear of his pants.

DOC
Got your twelve bullets now.

WYATT
You're so literal.

DOC
It's what keeps me breathing.

Wyatt exits.

Doc kicks back and relaxes.

DOC
Why couldn't I have been a gynecologist; Dentist fits way too easy on a bullet.
(to himself)
I'm changing my name to Nathaniel Zimmerman; or something equally long that would not even squeeze onto an Indian's tomahawk never mind some bullet that's waiting to introduce me to my *end of days.*

INT. TAILOR'S EMPORIUM DAY

Doc reaches to the Tailor's breast pocket.

DOC
May I?

The Tailor hesitates then nods.

Doc takes a tape measure from his pocket and lets it unwind all the way to the floor.

DOC

Thank you.

Measures the width of his own chest.

TAILOR

Not planning to be with us much longer?

DOC

Just the opposite. Any twine?

Tailor points to a ball of string.

INT. BLACKSMITH DAY

The Blacksmith looks up; the CLOCK reads 10:45 AM.

Two horseshoes hang from two of four nails.

A glowing horseshoe lifts from the furnace, receives two BANGS from his hammer then HISSES in a trough of water.

A WET horseshoe now drips from the third nail.

The Blacksmith uses tongs to grasp a small rod of iron.

DAYTONA (O.S.)

Hey Blacksmith.

He turns to see Daytona with a COIN on his thumbnail.

The Blacksmith deftly catches the coin CHINGING through the air.

DAYTONA

Make me a bullet. And remember to make it baby smooth by 12 noon.

MONTAGE

Places COIN into a ladle then the ladle onto some hot coals.

Liquid metal pours into the hole of a two-piece mould.

TAP TAP with a wooden hammer and the mould opens to reveal a bullet with burs.

Blacksmith looks to the CLOCK.

Clamps the bullet in a vice and starts filing it.

INT. HOTEL DAY

Shilling opens the curtains to let some light in. Upon the floor lay an open briefcase. A desk holds an array of etching tools. A small vice traps a single bullet already etched with the letters "D" and "A".

He sits and etches a "Y"... with room for further letters.

EXT. BARBERS DAY

Daytona enters the Barbers.

He tilts the Barber's mirror to reflect the entrance to the Hotel.

Barber reaches for mirror...

CLICK of Daytona's pistol at Barber's crotch.

DAYTONA
That's close enough.

BARBER
I wont take off more than I aught to.

DAYTONA
That's just how I like it.

INT/EXT. HOTEL DAY

Shilling leaves the Hotel and walks towards Barbers.

INT. BARBERS DAY

The door bell TINKLES.

Shilling walks right onto the end of Daytona's pistol.

CLICK-CLICK BANG!

EXT. BARBERS DAY

Shilling staggers out of the Barbers into the street and falls beside his own pistol.

Daytona stamps a boot upon the knuckles reaching out.

DAYTONA
(tutts)
I hear you're quite an engraver?

Shilling winces.

DAYTONA
I'm also known to dabble.

Twists boot causing him to wince more.

DAYTONA
You wanna see? Seeing as though I made it especially.

Daytona takes a coin (English Shilling) from his pocket.

DAYTONA
Give you three guesses.

Puts coin in his face and twists boot on his wrist.

SHILLING
(wincing)
A Shilling?

DAYTONA
Bravo.

Daytona takes out the specially minted bullet.

SHILLING
Made from a shilling?

Daytona's moustache twitches at the corner.

DAYTONA
I like you Mr. Shilling. I like your style.

Daytona takes Shilling's pistol, opens it up.

DAYTONA
Let me guess the first name. Hmmm, PEDRO? No, that's not me.

Balcony above Daytona CREAKS.

Daytona spins and fires up through the balcony.

PEDRO falls from the balcony.

DAYTONA
Pedro I presume?

The next bullet reads "Daytona".

The bullet bounces off Shillings face then lay in the dirt.

DAYTONA
My lucky day. Who says a man can't hold his own fate in his hand?

Loads the shiny bullet made from the English coin.

SHILLING
Confucius?

Daytona lowers the gun to Shilling's head. BANG.

Strikes a match on his boot and lights a cigar...

DAYTONA
That question was rhetorical.

INT. LAST CHANCE SALOON NIGHT

O'FLANNEL, an unkempt ginger Irishman with excess nasal hair looks to the floor where the anemic Doc stares at the ceiling. O'REIRDEN and O'CONNOR sport healthy beards. All members of the 'OH' gang wear long trench coats.

Doc regains his feet.

DOC

I am a keen fan of hygiene. And not particular to excessive growths; nasal hair especially. It blocks the respir'...respirator' respi'...

(sneezes)

...blocks the, nose.

Doc smiles.

DOC

Where as, I like to be in the best of health, as you can see.

Doc stumbles into O'Reirden and O'Connor.

DOC

Excuse me... aim me towards the bar please. Barman, please get myself and my new friends here a shot of your finest ginger ale. One for me, and one for these ginger men... I mean gentlemen.

MOMENTS LATER

O'Flannel, O'Reirden and O'Connor run into the street searching for something.

O'FLANNEL

Just where'd he go? No one's that fast.

SOON LATER...

INT/EXT. PHOTOSHOP NIGHT

CREAK of floorboard outside on the veranda.

O'Flannel's silhouette appears at the window.

Then a gun barrel pokes in round the opening door.

A sulphurous FLASH in his face of O'Flannel blinds him.

O'FLANNEL
WAHHH!

DOC
God that nostril hair's gotta be all short 'n' peachy.

Doc runs and hides.

MOMENTS LATER

INT. PHOTOSHOP NIGHT

The door creaks open.

Doc looks through a *flap* in the canvas backdrop, through a HANDSOME KNIGHT's VISOR in a depiction of SLEEPING BEAUTY.

Enter O'Connor, O'Flannel and O'Reirden.

O'CONNOR
Call it da luck o' da Irish, but it's like those eyes are just following me 'round da room.

O'REIRDEN
Your knight in shining armor.

Doc sees O'Flannel's burnt face down the end of a barrel.

DOC
Is this where I say cheese?

They all open fire. BANG BANG BANG Doc stumbles back onto his butt. A tight grouping of bullets puncture the depiction of the Knight's breastplate.

O'FLANNEL
And dee all lived happily ever after.

Laughter over smoking guns.

As the smoke clears...

Missy appears in a nightgown. Doc is beneath the canvas.

MOMENTS LATER

The Photographer and Missy unravel Doc.

Opening his perforated shirt reveals a dented *photo plate* held with heavy-duty string. The plate is a 'close up' NEGATIVE of Doc holding his chin.

Opening his eyes he rubs his chin.

DOC
I told you it was a close shave.
(beat)
This has gotta hurt in the morning.

EXT. FORT EDGE OF FRONTIER 4 DAYS LATER

Daytona rocks back and forth on his donkey for miles.

He rides right up to the POSTMAN sat outside and throws down a MAILBAG.

DAYTONA
Pony Express! I hope there's no perishables.

POSTMAN appears.

POSTMAN
The Pony Express doesn't come this way.

DAYTONA
It does now.

JACOBS, a uniformed soldier walks by.

DAYTONA
Hey, soldier, where you stationed?

JACOBS
Fort Atkinson. I'm Lieutenant Jacobs.

DAYTONA
Fort Atkinson? I think I got a letter from your momma.

Jacobs picks up the mailbag. Daytona pats him on the back.

DAYTONA
Sorry to hear about your dog. No news is good news as they say.

JACOBS
You read my mail?

DAYTONA
It was a long journey, I got bored. And I can't read too good. Now you got us *both* crying.

Jacobs riffles through the torn letters.

A sign reads "MEXICO THAT WAY".

Daytona looks to Jacobs then the sign.

DAYTONA
Need I ask how far?

EXT. DESERT MEXICAN BORDER DAY

The wind whips up a tumbleweed.

Daytona crouches over his lame Donkey.

A TWIG snaps underfoot. No-name stands with short toothpick.

Daytona spins round, his hand hovers over an empty holster.

DAYTONA
Huh?

No-name holds Daytona's gun.

NO NAME
Now what would a lame donkey be doing out here with a loser like you???

DAYTONA
You looking for someone mister? You going to shoot me with my own gun?

NO NAME
Tut-tut. In your delirium you've overlooked that your pony there seems to be in quite some pain.

Tumbleweed rolls by.

NO NAME
The nations who know this pass well say a *stink* blows towards Mexico. Anything that gets up my nose seems to also run that way.

DAYTONA
What is it you want?

No-name opens Daytona's pistol.

NO NAME
You don't happen to know anyone around here that's ran all the way from Marin County now do ya?

NO NAME
Five in the barrel?

No-name lets bullets drop to the floor.

NO NAME
Eenie, Meanie, Minie and now *Moe.*

The gun THUDS in the dirt at Daytona's feet.

NO NAME
Now we both know that leaves you only one bullet.
(beat)
But you got options. The way I figure this is; in a sick but satisfying game of Russian roulette, you can put your sick donkey out of its misery and then hop on over to Mexico hoping I just don't shoot you; or likewise risk having a shot at *me* with the knowledge that-that lame donkey will out live *your* sorry ass.

No-name CLICKS back the hammer on his pistol.

Daytona without breaking eye contact picks up the gun and slowly turns the barrel towards the Donkey's head.

CLICK-CLICK... CLUNK of an empty chamber.

No-name breathes in.

CLICK-CLICK... CLUNK.

Daytona squints.

Again... CLICK-CLICK... CLUNK.

NO NAME
It's getting kind-a tense aint it?

CLICK-CLICK... CLUNK

Daytona's eyes flit side to side.

CLICK-CLICK

Daytona and No-name stare intently at each other.

DAYTONA
You know what separates Saints from Sinners?

NO NAME
You plannin' takin' the answer to your grave?

Points to Mexican border with toothpick.

NO NAME
If that aint the route you plan on taking, who's gonna be tellin' your story?

Daytona sighs. BANG! The Donkey is put out of its misery.

LONG PAUSE

DAYTONA
You love animals or somethin'?

NO NAME
Somethin'.

Daytona turns slowly. Walks slowly towards Mexico.

NO NAME
You *know* reaching the Mexican border makes a free *man*?

DAYTONA
You don't say.

NO NAME
No, I said it. Take my advice, watch those double-negatives, one may get the wrong impression and not take too kindly to it.

DAYTONA
You a Saint?

NO NAME
No, I'm still planning on shooting. Just thinking how inconvenient dragging your corpse back would be.

MONTHS LATER

INT. HIGH COURT 'STATE VS. WYATT EARP' DAY

CITIZENS bustle into a packed out hall. JUDGE conducts all proceedings from his podium with an OFFICER at his side. The PROSECUTION resides left of center. Prosecution stands.

PROSECUTION
Your Honor. The State versus, Mr. Wyatt Earp.

JUDGE
The defendant?

OFFICER
Call the defendant.

WYATT EARP (bearded) enters and walks the long mile to the dock; puts his hand on the Bible in the Officer's hand.

OFFICER
Repeat after me. Do you swear by almighty god to tell the truth, the whole truth and nothing but the truth so help you god?

WYATT
Too fucking right I do.

Citizens gasp.

JUDGE
Quiet please.

Judge BANGS gavel, nods to the Officer.

OFFICER
Please confirm your name.

WYATT
Wyatt Earp.

CHIT CHATTER from court.

BANG BANG, gun like gavel from Judge.

JUDGE
I call for *order*! *Order*!

Judge motions to the paper shuffling PROSECUTION who brings a copy to the bench and hands it to the Judge.

PROSECUTION
Mr. Earp?

Wyatt stares.

PROSECUTION
February fifteenth, in the year of our lord 1876, mean anything to you?

WYATT
Not particularly.

PROSECUTION
How about Marin County?

WYATT
I heard of it.

PROSECUTION
A criminal outpouring... Inmates of Marin County; some one-thousand-men, broke out... and in what can only be described as an act of genocide; were systematically hunted down and slaughtered like cattle. How do you plea?

WYATT
Guilty.

All gasp.

The judge leans forward.

WYATT
Though, I can't take all the credit for it. I did have some help.

LATER IN THE PROCEEDINGS...

Doc and Calamity sit in the public gallery.

PROSECUTION
Is it *not* fair to say that this leader of the *Swarm*; this Daytona as you have named him; had what's commonly called a face-off, with a man with no name? And he was killed? Is it not so farfetched to assume that if one thousand men died by your hands. That he was shot too?

WYATT
I'd say that was a fair assumption, but it's not the truth.

JUDGE
Stop leading the jury.

PROSECUTION
Many men and women, led by the *then* acting Marshal, Mr. Earp here, seem to have been a law unto themselves. As an intelligent Jury, do you believe this man's tale? Or do you of sound mind think that this woven cacophony; this intricate story recorded by his own biographer, Stuart Lake be nothing more than the tallest of *said* Indian folklore fairytales?

JUDGE
Will the jury retire to make its' verdict?

WYATT
Can I speak your Honor?

Judge nods.

Wyatt stands and waits till all settle and are listening.

WYATT

The job of Marshalling this land has always been turned town by the tamest of men, and woman for that matter. And I of all people know that justice which ends in the death of one man let alone many - must have a trial and many of these trials are fraught with uncertainty.

(beat)

These citizens are baying for my blood. Let me tell you *Your Honor*, life is no cheaper in the *west* than in the *east*; though the availability of guns has made the shedding of one's blood a little easier.

(beat)

In my defense I want you to know that this land is a calmer place for what I and some others in this room were ordered to set in motion. Those who can *now* walk the *quiet* parks and play with their children in the *quiet* streets must remember one thing. In such a short time you forget that life was a lot wilder in the west. And yes, I was law unto myself, there was no one else.

(beat)

I don't know how easy your lives have become but it's a darn lot easier than any who still have to look over their shoulder 'cause they walk in moccasins.

(beat)

It's one mass slaughter. There are no more cows in cow city. No more food for the land of moccasined feet. This is slowly becoming no country for old men, so *you* think long and hard whether you want this neck-tie party to go ahead, or whether you'd give a man a chance and let a man run for his life like we did back in February 1876.

JUDGE
I would like to adjourn the proceedings till first thing tomorrow. I'm sure the Jury would like time to consider its final verdict?

JURY FOREMAN nods.

EXT. HIGH COURT 'STATE VS. WYATT EARP' DAY

Laborers erect a hangman's platform.

A smoke ring appears from beneath an onlooker's Sombrero.

ONLOOKER IS DAYTONA (V.O.)
Saints and Sinners? Now if I was to take the moral high ground, to go in there and tell the truth; he'd be a free man and I'd be the one with the noose round my neck.
(beat)
Who am I to take the moral high ground? Puts a man between a rock and a hard place.

Deep puff.

Throws down cigarette and twists boot over it.

He glances at the gallows noose and walks away.

Continues walking.

DAYTONA (V.O.)
Must be a hard call, judging the fine line between a *Saint and a Sinner*. The thought of an innocent man swinging sickens even *me* in the pit of my stomach. A last man's thought would be that nipping rope at his throat. Whether he's right or wrong I bet it stings like a bitch.

INT. HIGH COURT 'STATE VS. WYATT EARP' DAY

Wyatt cuts a fat cigar into shape and the attending Officer lights it.

WYATT
Much obliged. Thank you Your Honor.
(beat)
I never liked your *General Custer;* and after he promoted the mining of the *gold* Hills, *Sitting Bull* didn't like him either; it's his peoples' land, I saw the man's point, didn't take much to empathize, but that wasn't enough to justify any wanting the man dead.
(beat)
I along with the help of *others* waited in the hills with Sitting Bull; waiting for *The Swarm.*
(beat)
Then, Chaos... a *hell on Earth* is the only way to describe what happened next. We watched the two parties converge from our relatively safe vantage point. Custer's men and *The Swarm* were below cutting chunks out of each other. Yes there was a battle.
(beat)
As for the disgraced survivor...

EXT. EN ROUTE TO THE MEXICAN BORDER DAY

A mule trots along...

It's rider *General Custer,* wears a Sombrero.

The mule buckles underfoot.

MOMENTS LATER... CLICK-CLICK OF A PISTOL COCKING

NO NAME
Now we both know you got two options.

FLASH FORWARD TO THE PRESENT DAY

INT. SAN MARIN HIGH SCHOOL HISTORY CLASS DAY

Young-Quentin stands behind his WILD WEST diorama. Miss Prairie gives a sign to wrap up his presentation.

YOUNG QUENTIN
(SIGHS)
And so the sun set for the last time for Mr. Earp. The town in which he was *tried* became nothing more than a ghost town. Many Bounty Hunter's that came from afar were buried in them hills. Wyatt was never again to look from that City Marshal's Office.
(beat)
His memoirs, told to biographer Stuart Lake recorded only a sense of what truly happened and a few posters remain.

School BELL RINGS. A few chairs screech.

MISS PRAIRIE
One moment!

Miss Prairie taps her pen upon her clipboard. The whole class claps and cheers.

MISS PRAIRIE
Quentin, you certainly know how to tell the tallest of tales; and a wild one at that.

Screech of chairs.

MISS PRAIRIE
A paragraph on the *WILD WEST*'s law makers or breakers! Usual number of words by Monday.

Pupils groan.

MINUTES LATER EVERY PUPIL HAS GONE

Miss Prairie collects the text books from each desk.

Beneath the Wild West DIORAMA lay Quentin's old PONY EXPRESS mailbag.

Moments later, in her hands... A sepia photograph and on the table a pair of Wild West SPURS.

MISS PRAIRIE
Oh my. Surely not.

She flicks her eyebrows upwards.

MOMENTS LATER...

INT. STAFFROOM SAN MARIN HIGH SCHOOL DAY

Miss Prairie leans against the PHOTOCOPIER apple in hand.

The copier flashes and chugs into motion.

She lifts a COPY from the TRAY and laughs hysterically; and bites hard into the apple.

CLOSE ON: Chicago Herald article: A man's ass with a colorful SIOUX handprint on each buttock. Across his chest he wears a banner. "I BEAT THE BOUNTY".

MISS PRAIRIE
Naked Spurs?

She chuckles. In the OUT TRAY lands copy upon copy of the bare man's BUTTOCKS.

An old letter in her hand reads:

MISS PRAIRIE
To the man I call a friend.

She unfolds the letter inside.

FLASHBACK TO 1876

EXT. BLACK HILLS SUNSET

A campfire flickers amongst the towering sandstone buttes.

INDIAN CHILDREN sit listening to Chief-Sitting-Bull.

SITTING BULL
(in Cheyenne accent)
In this very place,
the distant sound of...

MISS PRAIRIE (V.O.)
(storytelling)
In this very place,
the distant sound of...

SITTING BULL
...spurs traveled like a wind
through the hills.
(beat)
Then he appeared, the man who could
run swift like horse.

Chief-Sitting-Bull points to the horizon.

SITTING BULL
The man with no gun, looking not
for a fight, but for freedom.

MATCH CUT TO:

AUTHOR'S FOOTNOTE:

Flick through THUMBNAIL images (top right) to see the envisioned MATCH CUT transition.

EXT. SITTING BULL MONUMENT SUNSET, PRESENT DAY

Reveal the sun at the fingertip of the gargantuan rock carving that is Sitting Bull.

The carved face of Sitting Bull stares down an outstretched arm upon which stand Miss Prairie with a group of students from San Marin High School.

SITTING BULL (V.O.)	MISS PRAIRIE
(Cheyenne accent)	(reading)
You too may one day bring your children...	You too may one day bring your children...

MISS PRAIRIE
...to this very spot and one day tell them of the same swift-footed man, the legend of laughter we have named as *Naked Spurs*.

POV RISING LIKE A BIRD INTO THE SKY.

MISS PRAIRIE
You are welcome here anytime; your appearance will bring many years of great merriment to our children and our children's children. You will not be forgotten.
(beat)
Your good friend, Sitting Bull.

THE GHOSTLY SOUND OF SPURS PEAKS AND THEN FADES.

THE LOVELY LAUGHTER OF SITTING BULL ECHOES.

FADE OUT:

THE END

STORY EPILOGUE
(continues on p.99)

Search for Eurydice
SEARCH FOR EURYDICE
GREEK TRAGEDY
"The most famous Orphic tale"
Two GODS wager on whether one man can succeed in the present
...and rescue his wife from the Underworld
... she's not quite dead yet!
Screenplay and Graphic Novel by KARL SMITH
ARGONAUTS once searched for
..."THE GOLDEN FLEECE"
- Orpheus
Their SEARCH continues...
HERMES
Vs.
APHRODITE
Based upon the most famous Orphic tale:
SEARCH FOR EURYDICE
Screenplay & Graphic Novel
KARL SMITH
(uri-dee-chee)
Screenplay
2 in 1
OF MEN AND MYTH
Graphic Novel
(STORYBOARD)
SCREENPLAY & GRAPHIC NOVEL

"If you completely storyboard a movie you neuter possibilities for happy accidents"
- Gore Verbinski, *Director of Pirates of the Caribbean: Curse of the Black Pearl.*

A story that will appeal to general readers and classicists alike.

When the reputations of two gods hinge on the actions of one man expect all hell to break loose when gun-toting Argonauts descend all-guns-blazing to the Underworld.

Orpheus's wife is not quite dead yet!

He must find her.

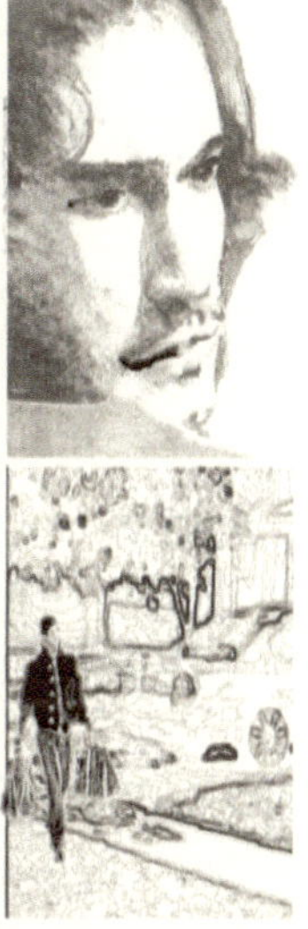

"Clutching my sister, heavy, dead in my arms; my cries for help drowned out by the music of the Pool hall. One Greek hero had been here before me; Orpheus."
- Karl Peter Smith, *The Author.*

email: orphichouse@yahoo.co.uk   titles available from all good book stores

Greek mythology
Comic book, strips
Graphic Novels

FICTION

SEARCH FOR EURYDICE:
SCREENPLAY AND GRAPHIC NOVEL

HARDBACK
ISBN 978-0-9566156-6-4

PAPERBACK
ISBN 978-0-9566156-0-2

BOOK SIZE: US LETTER 8"x11.5"

KARL SMITH

Serial Pool Attendant
SCREENPLAY
WRITTEN BY KARL SMITH
Alexandra Vino
Brian Spangler
TV PILOT & SERIES BIBLE
Keeping L.A. clean is just MURDER.
* Includes the 24 PAGE 'Bible' for the TV Series. L.A. Serial Pool
A minute by minute breakdown of the 'Hero's Journey' for TV.
(p.84-107.)
Four-Act Structure, where Act breaks match commercial breaks.
An insight into ABC, CBS, NBC, FOX, and new BBC TV format.
Serial Pool

SERIAL POOL ATTENDANT

Synopsis:
On an L.A. beach Alex (pool attendant) meets her idol, the notorious Shark (real name Henry, a high profile killer on parole). Shark mentors Alex in the art of 'murder' and in 'not getting caught'. Cultural references lead to his catchphrase . . .

"A CLASSIC!"

The big reveal: Shark is not just a serial killer but a puppet taking orders from Victoria (once screenplay tutor to Alex) and mission director of an assassin-like organisation known as the . . .

'SERIAL POOL'

It is not mere chance that brings Alex and Henry together.

Siblings with a flair for death. Shark takes his sister under his wing.

Hitmen liaising as *real CLEANERS.*

"IF YOUR PROBLEM IS TOO BIG TO FILTER . . .YOU CALL THE POOL ATTENDANT"

Concept:
Two loyal Psycho's team up to create the L.A. version of "Miami Vice". Add a sexy mission director... Victoria... a sprinkling of "Mission Impossible" and that's ENTERTAINMENT!

"YOU'LL DIE LAUGHING"

"...lunatic brother-sister psychology at its finest."

About the Author
Karl Smith graduated with a degree in Fine Art from Cleveland College of Art and Design. His fresh fusion of action and emotion when screenwriting is surely to be seen in a cinema near you soon. Bet your mortgage on it!

ASK YOUR LOCAL BOOK STORE TO STOCK OTHER ORPHIC HOUSE TITLES

SERIAL POOL ATTENDANT:
SCREENPLAY & TV SERIES BIBLE

HARDBACK
ISBN 978-0-9566156-7-1

PAPERBACK
ISBN 978-0-9566156-2-6

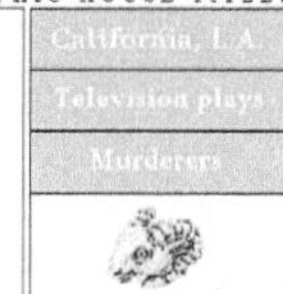

A HISTORY OF FEAR

"Will put the frighteners up you."

"A GRIPPING TALE!"

חי

Raya Baumann's

A HISTORY OF FEAR

SCREENPLAY

BONUS MATERIAL: ALTERNATE ENDINGS

WRITTEN BY KARL SMITH "... A FAIRY-TALE HORROR."

A HISTORY OF FEAR

Synopsis:
A wish melds the soul of a kind-hearted simpleton to a toy BEAR. A secret for three generations, the seven foot GUARDIAN wakes in time of need.

Surviving the sinking of the TITANIC a toy BEAR passes into the hands of the JEWISH COMMUNITY. Aboard the rescue ship CARPATHIA it travels on to the gas chambers of AUSCHWITZ.

The BEAR brings something with it…A HISTORY OF FEAR.

When TRICK OR TREATERS uncover an SS OFFICER in the neighborhood . . .

HALLOWEEN IS ABOUT TO GET A LITTLE HAIRY

Concept:
'Gremlins' meets 'Schindler's List' / 'The Golem of Prague'.

Teddy bears
Juvenile drama
Jewish faith

ORPHIC HOUSE

A HISTORY OF FEAR:
SCREENPLAY

HARDBACK
ISBN 978-0-9566156-9-5

PAPERBACK
ISBN 978-0-9566156-3-3

KARL SMITH

 - A touching sweet story up-there with the tallest of tales.

"ENJOYABLE. LAUGH-OUT-LOUD"

NAKED SPURS

SCREENPLAY

"*Wyatt Earp* was well known for telling seriously tall tales."

- STUART LAKE, BIOGRAPHER

a tall-tale worth every bit it's weight in gold

WRITTEN BY KARL SMITH

"No one gets their <u>drawers</u> off faster in the WEST."

"Naked but for a pair of spurs"

"Did one man truely outwit the greatest gunslingers in history?"

"I do sincerely wish it were tru

- California 1876 -

NAKED SPURS

"NO ONE GETS THEIR DRAWERS OFF FASTER IN THE WEST"

CALIFORNIA 1876

A COAST MIWOK WARRIOR AND THE PRISON THAT WAS TO BE NAMED AFTER HIM

Saint ...  *... Quentin*

YOUNG ARTIST creates a Wild West diorama and tells the seriously tall tale of AKED SPURS, his great-great grandfather.

AKED SPURS is the plausible tale of the BEAT THE BOUNTY competition ontest attracting the fastest guns in the West to the largest manhunt in history.

the streaking inmate of San Quentin penitentiary NAKED SPURS must run for his along with other criminals.

This is one story he cannot run away from.

FROM THE MAN WITH BALLS IS BORN A LEGEND."

ıspiration:

yatt Earp told his memoirs to his biographer Stuart Lake.
one story he was suspected of fixing a prize fight in which he was the judge.
ıe book was suspected to be entirely fictional.

oncept:

he Good, the Bad and the Ugly' meets '*My name is Earl*' ... well, Earp actually.

About the Author
Karl Smith graduated with a degree in Fine Art from Cleveland College of Art and Design. His fresh fusion of action and emotion when screenwriting is surely to be seen in a cinema near you soon. Bet your mortgage on it!

HARDBACK
THE SOUND OF NAKED SPURS:
A SPAGHETTI WESTERN SCREENPLAY
ISBN 978-0-9566156-8-8

PAPERBACK
NAKED SPURS: SCREENPLAY
ISBN 978-0-9566156-2-6

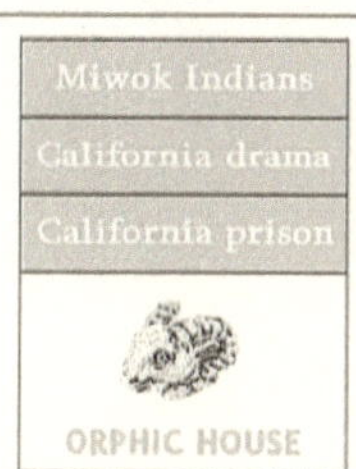

Purge
the Soul
screenplay
written by
KARL SMITH

Memoirs of Dirty Max
Screenplay
written by
Karl Smith

'Moving words around a page is like painting.'

To learn this process check out... Print-on-demand Technical Guide: Screenplay Publishing

Screenplay Resume

Artwork

Karl Peter Smith

E-PORTFOLIO:

1. Search for Eurydice - Romance with Bite
2. Serial Pool Attendant - Crime
3. Naked Spurs - Western
4. A History of Fear - Horror
5. Purge the Soul – Thriller
6. Memoirs of Dirty Max - Romance
7. Bikini THREE-20 (Thunderbirds) – Sci-Fi
8. Bill and Ted's Idiot's Guide to Screenwriting - Comedy

EDUCATION

UNIVERSITY OF TEESSIDE, Cleveland, England.
Bachelor of Fine Art - Printing, Drawing and Painting.
Specialized in Sculpture

HONOURS

Cleveland College of Art and Design used my sculptures to advertise the college in the UCAS prospectus; a national publication attracting future students to campus.

"I cried whilst writing."

A History Of Fear

"...the blonde ponytail."

Thanks Helen x

Pencil Drawing of Miss. Helen Shepley by K.S. 2006

Epilogue...

FADE IN:

INT. HIGH COURT DAY

Citizens wait in a packed out hall. Judge enters and takes his podium. Prosecution left of center.

JUDGE
Call the defendant please.

OFFICER
Call the defendant!

Enter Wyatt with a long drawn out walk.

Wyatt leans back on his chair. His single action six-shooter falls from his holster to the floor and discharges.

BANG!

The bullet goes through his coat and out through the ceiling.

Citizens gasp.

WYATT
(coyly)
I find it just a little embarrassing.
Can we omit that from the record?

FADE OUT:

THE END

"The story of a sound, sounds like a great story."

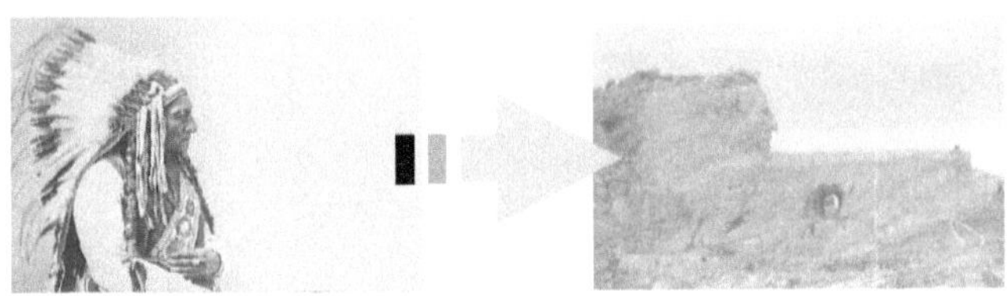

ROLL CREDITS

LYRICAL BARD (Vanessa Paradis)

Picture *Vanessa Paradis* rising in a Hot Air Baloon.
Singing as the credits rise...

Alizée's - Mes courants électriques / Gourmandises

Author's note:

Even though I do not know the words
the beauty of the song and the singer,
and the moment it evokes
is multi-cultural

Listen, and be seduced.

DAYTONA (Johnny Depp)

The *Captain Jack Sparrow* of the *Wild West.*

END CREDITS

(continued from page 'v')

"WYATT EARP"

Part two.

Died age 80 on January 13, 1929.

He left no children.

Grief stricken
Josephine Sarah Marcus (his Jewish wife)
had Earp's body cremated
and his ashes buried
in the Marcus family plot
'HILLS OF ETERNITY'
Colma, California.

15 years later
Josie's ashes were buried...
...next to Earp's.

R.I.P.

www.ingramcontent.com/pod-product-compliance
Lightning Source LLC
Chambersburg PA
CBHW020615310726
48979CB00008B/1490/J

* 9 7 8 0 9 5 6 6 1 5 6 8 8 *